The Celtic Spider

David Scott

Email: davidarts@eircom.net
Phone: +353 87 759 6715
www.davidscott.ie

For Mick McMahon

The Celtic Spider
by
David Scott

Dramatis Personae

Jean
Susan (Jean's sister)
Father
Uncle
Mother
Her Lover
Bartender
McManus
Romanian
Traveler 1
Traveler 2
Fairy 1
Fairy 2
Cuchulain
Holly
The Doctor
Annie Fanny
Assistant
Garda

This play was originally performed accompaied by the music of Michael and Matthew McMahon from the album The Well Travelled Melody with their kind permission. It is not a stipulation that this music be used in production, however renewed permission must be sought if this music is desired.

The Celtic Spider

ACT I
Scene 1

Cuchulain is dead, bound to the rock. His head is down. Downstage left Jean stands alone. His mother stands upstage with her lover. Jean's father center right. Susan stands up left. Down right is the uncle in a priest's collar.

Sign: The Beast of Death.

(Lights down on all as they exit except Jean.)

Jean: A piece of red tape tied between two trees.

(His father re-enters and wanders across the stage. He seems lost.)

Father: My head has not gone down. My head is high.

(The sound of a crow. Wind. The Stage is swept with darkness. Two Faeries enter.)

Fairy 1: Well, it's been a long time.

Fairy 2: It has. A hundred years or more.

Fairy 1: More, I'd say. Think about it. When was the last time?

Fairy 2: In the time of the heroes.

Fairy 1: Yes. And that was a long time ago.

Fairy 2: I don't like to leave the river and come to this place.

Fairy 1: Me either.

Fairy 2: There's something smelly about the place. Have you noticed?

Fairy 1: Noticed? It stinks. It smells of dust and smoke. Before there was offal and fires and sometimes rotting flesh, but not this smell. It's a smell of decay.

Fairy 2: Rotting flesh is decay, you stupid fairy.

Fairy 1: A decay of the air itself, I mean.

Fairy 2: Let's go home. I feel weak here. I can't breathe properly.

Fairy 1: No. We have to take the human child with us.

Fairy 2: What human child?

Fairy 1: The one who sees past the objects. The one who can see us.

Fairy 2: Where will we find this one?

Fairy 1: In the same place. The village. It is always the village they live in. I have met with her before. Fairies visit her occasionally.

Fairy 2: There are so many villages now. So many houses.

Fairy 1: Must be a housing boom.

Fairy 2: Looks like it.

Fairy 1: We'll find her. Apparently she likes crisps.

Fairy 2: What are crisps?

Fairy 1: *(Presenting a packet of crisps.)* I bought a pack for research purposes.

Fairy 2: Ooooh.

(Fairy 1 opens the crisps. Fairy 2 takes one and eats it.)

Fairy 2: That's fucking horrible.

Fairy 1: *(Eating a crisp and spitting it out.)* What does she want with these things?

Fairy 2: Satisfaction apparently.

Fairy 1: What kind of satisfaction do you get from that?

Fairy 2: Their taste buds must have devolved in some way.

Fairy 1: Or ours needed to and didn't.

Fairy 2: Let us not eat the crisps. I fear for the girth of our bums.

Fairy 1: Agreed.

Fairy 2: I really don't feel well.

Fairy 1: No. Me either. We must find the girl and get out of here. Back to the river.

Fairy 2: Yes. At the river there is only freshness.

Scene 2

The characters move to the living room and seat themselves. They stare into the audience.

Uncle: There's nothing on. Switch it off.

Father: I'll switch you off.

Mother: Shut up, both of you.

(Pause.)

Jean: Susan's hungry.

Mother: Susan, are you hungry?

Susan: No.

Mother: Jean, get Susan some crisps.

Susan: I'm not hungry.

Mother: Eat the crisps.

Jean: She doesn't want any.

Mother: Have you gone yet?

Jean: She doesn't want any crisps.

Mother: Get her a packet of crisps.

Jean: Susan, are you hungry? Do you want crisps?

Susan: Yes.

Jean: I'll go and get them.

(He goes.)

Uncle: I'm off to bed.

Father: Good.

Mother: Leave him be, Bill.

Father: I don't have the energy to not leave him be.

Mother: Very mysterious. Very abstract.

Father: I thought you'd like it.

(Jean returns with crisps. He gives them to Susan.)

Susan: Open them. I can't open the crisps.

Jean: Yes you can. I've seen you do it.

Susan: I can't tonight.

Jean: Why?

Susan: Do it. Open the crisps.

Jean: You do it.

(Suddenly Susan squeezes the bag and it bursts open.)

Jean: Shit.

Mother: Now look what you made her do. Clean it up.

(No one moves. Susan eats the crisps that have fallen on her. A knock.)

Mother: Get the door, Jean.

(A pause. Jean gets up and goes to the door.)

Uncle: I'm tired and afraid.

Father: Idiot.

(Jean enters with a Romanian immigrant. He holds a card with writing on it. He passes it to Jean.)

Jean: I am from Romania. My child has leukemia… he spelt it wrong… I need money for her to be treated in proper hospital. Please help. God will go with you.

(Silence.)

Jean: What should I do?

Father: Give him a Euro.

Mother: What if he's lying? He could be after heroin.

Father: Give him a fucking Euro or he'll come back and burgle the place.

(Jean reaches into his pocket and pulls out a Euro. He hands it to the Romanian.)

Romanian: Thank you. Thank you. God is to your house and in its home.

Jean: Come on. I'll see you out. You'll never get past the locks.

(Jean sees him out.)

Uncle: God is not in this house.

Father: *(To Uncle.)* I thought you were going to bed.

Uncle: I may well do. But I'm afraid to go to my attic loft.

Father: Why? What's there to be afraid of, huh? What?

Uncle: Death. What do you think?

Father: It'll get you anyway.

Uncle: It'll get you first.

Father: Don't count on it.

Mother: Shut up. They're about to screw.

Jean: *(Reentering.)* Mother, please turn that off. It's offensive.

Mother: It's material for you to masturbate by. Watch and learn.

Jean: It's sordid.

Mother: It's pornography. It's the most popular form of entertainment in the world. It makes three times what Hollywood makes. Store it up for your lonesome future.

Jean: I don't need to store it up.

Mother: Then what do you use to masturbate by if you have no pornographic memory?

Jean: I think of water.

(Pause.)

Mother: Very poetic. Very abstract.

Jean: Yes.

Susan: I think of Jean.

Jean: You do not, Susan.

Susan: Yes I do.

Jean: No, you don't.

Susan: I do.

Jean: Don't.

Susan: Do so.

Jean: Do not.

Father: End it!

(Silence.)

Jean: You're a fat weirdo.

Susan: You're a skinny spider.

Jean: Whatever.

Susan: Whatever yourself.

Mother: You're right, Jean. This screwing is most unsatisfactory.

Jean: Turn it off.

Father: I'm going to the pub.

Mother: Sit down.

(He exits. The Uncle goes to his room.)

Mother: In the morning I'm leaving early.

Jean: Yes Mother.

Mother: Put Susan to bed.

Jean: Come on, Susan.

Susan: Okay.

(They exit and watch the porn as they go.
Mother alone. She takes out a mobile phone, dials.)

Mother: Hi sexy. Are you watching channel twelve?

(Darkness but for the fairies.)

Fairy 1: That was her.

Fairy 2: Such beauty. I've never seen the like of it. A child of the natural world. A seer. She does not belong at all.

Fairy 1: It is most strange.

Scene 3

Sign: The Bartender at the End of the Rainbow

Bar. Female Bartender. Two travelers. Father.

Bartender: Another?

Father: No. Yes.

Bartender: Which is it?

Father: What do you think I should do?

Bartender: I'll get you another.
(Pause. She gets him a drink.)
You've been coming here twenty-five years and you still ask me that same question.

Father: I still don't know the answer.

Bartender: I know. You still love me?

Father: No.

Traveler 1: You want to buy carpet? I got carpet.

Father: No.

Traveler 2: It's good carpet. Go on. It's good. It's in the van. I'll get it.

Father: Don't get it.

Traveler 2: You want sheets? Kids sheets?

Father: What?

Traveler 1: For the bed. The kid's beds.

Father: I don't want it.

Traveler 2: Good price. Cheap.

Father: No.

Traveler 2: You want a fuckin… whatsit?

Father: A whatsit? What's a whatsit?

Traveler 2: A fucking camera. Video. Digital. All the bits and pieces.

Father: No. Yes.

Traveler 1: You do? A grand.

(He shows the camera.)

Father: I've got three hundred.

Traveler 1: Done.

(They exchange.)

Traveler 1: You want pants? I got pants.

Father: I bought your fucking camera. Now I'm going to buy you both a drink and in exchange you're going to leave me in peace while I have a drink. Okay?

Traveler 2: Right boss.

(The bartender serves them whiskey. They shut up.)

Father: You lads never sell pots anymore.

(The travelers don't speak.)

Father: You used to sell pots and pans. My father bought a bunch once and they had holes in them. He tracked down the tinker and boxed him. The tinker boxed him back and he wound up with a pin in his jaw for the rest of his life.

Bartender: They won't answer. They're men of their word.

Father: Their word? What's their word?

Bartender: They're men of their word.

Father: Are you still in love with me?

Bartender: No.

Father: Well that's something, I guess. At least we don't have to put up with that shit anymore.

Bartender: That's right. It was nothing but trouble.

(Pause.)

Bartender: How's your wife?

Father: She hates me.

Bartender: You're an idiot.

Father: Everybody's an idiot.

(Pause.)

Father: I still think you're beautiful.

Bartender: Everybody's beautiful.

Scene 4

Sign: The Stain of McManus

Site office. Jean, his Father and Mr McManus.

McManus: Bill. Are you working hard?

Father: Very hard, Mr McManus. We're painting like there's no tomorrow over there.

McManus: Good. You'll be paid greatly and with great wads of notes and things for this. And there's more where that came from.

Father: Thank you, Mr McManus.

McManus: How long have you been painting houses, Bill?

Father: Twenty-eight years, Mr McManus.

McManus: Well fuck, man. Aren't you bored yet?

Father: Mmmm.

McManus: I'd be bored out of my tits if I had to paint houses every feckin day. I'd want to blow my head off.

Father: But you're a contractor. Doesn't contracting bore you also, Mr McManus? No offence or anything like that intended.

McManus: Yes. I suppose it does. But I make assloads of money.

Father: Well I do too, sir.

McManus: Oh, do you?

Father: Well, not as much as…

McManus: I bet you don't make as many assloads as I do.

Father: Perhaps not, but I make enough to feed my family and be comfortable.

McManus: Is that all you want? To pump your money at your fucking family who don't give a shitty old boot about you?

Father: My family cares about me, sir. I don't mind spending my money on them.

McManus: Do they? Do they care?

Father: Yes.

McManus: Check that. Check that thoroughly.
  But enough about your stupid feckin' family. When will you be finished that house?

Father: Tomorrow evening, I think.

McManus: Good. Have it finished by the end of the day.

Father: Mr McManus, I wanted to check with you that the contract for the painting of the new estates is going to be mine. I feel I've earned…

McManus: Sure, sure. We'll talk.

(A pause. McManus waits. Jean and Father exit.)

Father: We have to finish it by the end of the day.

Jean: That's impossible.

Father: Not if we skip the undercoat on the living room.

Jean: But that would be dishonest.

Father: That would be pragmatic.

Jean: It would?

Father: And quicker.

Jean: Yes, I can see how it could be quicker.

(Pause.)

Father: Your uncle wants to see you tonight in his den.

Jean: What about?

Father: He said he wanted to see you?

Jean: What about?

Father: He said he wanted to see you.

Jean: What about?

Father: He said he wanted to see you.

(Pause.)

Father: You're a big lad, Jean. Big enough and ugly enough to look after yourself. You wouldn't let him molest you, would you?

Jean: No.
Have you had lunch?

Father: I'm not hungry.
My head went down, didn't it?

Jean: I didn't see it go down.

Father: It fell. I felt it in my neck.

Scene 5

Sign: The Creepy Crawly Uncle

Uncle holds a jar with a spider in it.

Jean: It is a spider.

Uncle: It is a spider.

Jean: What of it?

Uncle: What of it? What of you?

(Pause.)

Jean: Yes. What of me?

(Pause.)

Uncle: You are a measly anti-warrior. A phlegmy stain on a pair of old man's pants.

Jean: Yes, uncle.

Uncle: It's more than a spider. It's a poisonous spider.

Jean: There are no poisonous spiders in Ireland.

Uncle: Again you are wrong. In fact you are an error.

Jean: Yes Uncle.

Uncle: It is poisonous because I have exposed it to a radioactive, sub atomic substance that I scraped off the walls of my very own particle accelerator. This substance has enhanced this little fellow's natural venom and made it the most poisonous spider of all. If you are bitten by it you will die so quickly you will not even know you are dying. You will be dead before you know you are dead and in fact you will be dead even before your body is aware that death is coming. Indeed you will be dead faster than the time death takes to recognize the fact that it is death.

Jean: Goodness…

Uncle: You will be dead so fast, you won't know what death is… and neither will death.

(Pause.)

Jean: Goodness…

Uncle: Goodness. Is that all you have to say, you millipede?

Jean: Yes Uncle. Sorry Uncle.

(Enter mother.)

Mother: Jean, you are to look after your sister tonight. I have to go out.

Jean: But I looked after her last night. I've looked after her every night of the week this week and last week. I'd like some time to myself.

Mother: There will be plenty of time for yourself. You wait and see. Loneliness will engulf you like a plague and eat you whole.

(Pause.)

Jean: Yes mother.

Mother: Your father is a cretin and I can't trust him with the child. But he will be there too. Perhaps he will give you some time to yourself… to wank off.

(She exits.)

Jean: *(Aside.)* Fuck me.

Uncle: Yes, fuck you, Jean. Fuck you. Now take off your pants.

Jean: Uncle, you know I'm not going to take off my pants.

Uncle: Yes, yes, I know. Now get out of my laboratory before I smash your head in with the butt of a pistol.

Jean: You have a pistol?

Uncle: Of course I have a pistol.

Jean: May I see it?

Uncle: No. Be gone.

(Jean exits.)

Uncle: *(Quietly.)* Come back.

Scene 6

Sign: The Fact of Susan

Jean alone, wanking. His sister enters.

Susan: What are you doing Jean?

Jean: Christ! Get out!

Susan: Are you having a wank? Mother said you were looking for some time alone to have a wank.

Jean: Yes, I'm having a wank if you must know. Now get out!

Susan: What does wanking mean?

Jean: I'm not going to explain it to you just now. Go away.

Susan: Can I watch?

Jean: No!

Susan: Why not?

Jean: Because wanking is private. I thought father was watching you.

Susan: He walked away.

Jean: Again?

Susan: Yes. He just got up and walked away. Aimlessly he walked. I don't know where. Perhaps he made a phone call.

Jean: Why? Who did he need to call?

Susan: I don't know.

Jean: Then why did you say that?

Susan: He said he was feeling sick.

Jean: When? Just now?

Susan: My feet hurt. My knees hurt.

Jean: It's because you're standing for so long. Your weight is hurting your legs. Go and sit down and watch the fairies and I'll be there in a moment. I'll sit with you and I won't walk away.

Susan: But they hurt now.

Jean: Fine. *(He zips up.)* My balls are going to ache like hell for this.

(They go and sit.)

Susan: I can't see the fairies.

Jean: Why not?

Susan: I don't know. I can see them usually. But they're gone. The fairies are gone.

Jean: *(Quietly.)* I know.

(Enter Father.)

Father: Son, tomorrow we paint the third estate.

Jean: Yes Father.

Father: It will bring us great wealth, this job.

Jean: Yes.

Father, you know you can't leave Susan on her own.

Father: Did I leave her on her own?

Jean: You did. She came looking for me. Now her feet and knees hurt her.

Susan: They don't hurt me anymore.

Jean: But they were hurting you before, weren't they?

Susan: *(Pause.)* No.

Father: Jean, you really tell too many lies. We should have brought you up a Catholic. We made a mistake there… thought your freedom to choose your way was more important, but you've ended up a lying imp.

Jean: Yes Father.

Father: Why don't you go to bed and have a wank? I'll watch Susan.

Jean: But you won't. You'll walk away again.

Father: Yes, you're quite right.

Jean: I'll wait until she wants to sleep.

Susan: Perhaps the fairies will come back.

Father: Fucking fairies. What are you, retarded?

Jean: Yes father, she is retarded. Don't speak to her like that.

Father: Retarded, ey? I never noticed.

(Father walks off aimlessly. The lights fall. A Beat. They rise again. Susan is awake. Jean is asleep. Susan watches the fairies.)

Fairy 1: Come, Susan.

Susan: You have a new friend.

Fairy 2: Come with us.

Susan: No. That's okay. I just like to watch you. You're very pretty.

Fairy 1: Leave this place. Come with us.

Susan: Where?

Fairy 2: To the river. To the Boyne.

Susan: Why?

Fairy 1: The sadness here is too great. Come with us. We know a beautiful place to play.

Susan: I'll think about it.

Fairy 1: Come now.

Susan: Not yet. I have to see more yet. There is more to be gleaned. There is plenty of time for play.

Fairy 1: Time is not time, Susan.

Susan: I don't understand.

Fairy 2: Time only affects you because you are flesh. Forget about your flesh.

Susan: But there's so much of it.

Fairy 1: It doesn't mean anything.

Fairy 2: Come.

Susan: I will. But not yet.

Fairy 2: Death is coming.

(The fairies fly away. Susan turns to Jean. She undoes his fly and looks into his pants. Jean dreams. Cuchulain comes to Jean in his sleep.)

Cuchulain: What has become of you?

Jean: I don't know.

Cuchulain: Do you know who I am?

Jean: The son of Suiltim.
That's all I remember from school

Cuchulain: Do you know of my deeds?

Jean: Yes. You are a myth.

Cuchulain: Am I?

Jean: I think so.

Cuchulain: What are you doing? Why are you alive?

Jean: To… to live. To have life.

Cuchulain: But you're not doing anything with it.

Jean: What am I meant to do with it?

Cuchulain: Seize its throat.

Jean: But why?

Cuchulain: Because it is your enemy. You must conquer it.

Jean: Conquer what?

Cuchulain: The enemy.

Jean: What enemy?

Cuchulain: The enemy you cannot see.

Jean: How can I conquer an enemy I can't see?

Cuchulain: By smell.
Leave them.

Jean: How can I? My sister needs me. My father needs me to work with him.

Cuchulain: *(Roars like a lion.)* PAINTING?!

Jean: Your roar is frightening.

Cuchulain: All warriors have a war cry.

Jean: Do they?

Cuchulain: Of course. Show me your war cry.

(Pause. Jean stares blankly at him.)

Cuchulain: Where is the warrior in you?

Jean: I don't need to be a warrior. We are at peace.

Cuchulain: Do you need a war to be a man?

Jean: I am a man.

Cuchulain: You are a slave.

Jean: A slave? To what?

Cuchulain: To everything.

Jean: You. You were a slave. To women… to fate.

Cuchulain: Yes. I suppose you're right. There is nothing to be done.

Jean: Why are you here?

Cuchulain: I wish I knew.
(Pause.)
Leave this place or die.
And wake up. Your sister is looking at your penis.

(He exits. Jean notices Susan peering into his pants.)

Jean: What are you doing?

Scene 7

Sign: The Intrusion of the Lover

Mother: What time is it?

Lover: Seven.

Mother: I should go.

Lover: Don't go.

Mother: Why not? What's there to stay for?

(Pause.)

Mother: It's raining.

Lover: It's always raining.

Mother: It never makes anything clean. It only fouls it up. It makes it muddier. Dirtier. Water is meant to be pure.

Lover: I love you.

(Mother laughs hysterically.)

Mother: You do not, you fucking idiot. Where's my fucking pants.

(She begins to dress.)

Lover: I knew that would scare you. You love me too. You just won't admit it to yourself.

Mother: For fuck's sake, child. I don't love you. I love bits of you.

Lover: No. You can't do what we do and not feel a connection.

Mother: What if I told you I do this with two other guys, not including my husband as well and don't feel a connection to any of them... or you.

(Pause.)

Lover: I wouldn't believe you.

Mother: Listen to me, sexy. Don't shut your eyes. I had my eyes shut for a long time. I got married. I did as I was told. Then I ended up with a dysfunctional husband and a pair of really fucked up children who hate me. I was supposed to sit there and deal with that for the rest of my life. No. No more connections.
(Pause.)
There's no such thing as love. It's a trick of nature. It's designed to fool you into spawning more vermin.

If I walked out of here right now and never saw you again, you'd have me out of your head in three weeks and you'd be sniffing at someone else's crotch. .

Lover: No.

Mother: Yes.

(She has gathered up her things and heads for the door.)

Lover: If you don't love them, why don't you leave them? You could come and live with me.

Mother: I don't want to live with you. And I don't not love them. I just don't love them. Because love doesn't exist. Get it?

Lover: No.

Mother: Goodbye. Will I see you Thursday?

Lover: I don't have a choice.

Mother: You always have a choice. But every option is pain. Will I see you?

Lover/Mother: Thursday.

(Pause.)

Lover: Don't get wet.

Mother: I hate water.

Lover: You mean you hate the rain.

Mother: No. I hate water.

(She exits.)

Scene 8

Sign: Cuchulain on the M50.

The car on the way to work. Father is driving.

Jean: Father, slow down.

Father: Foreigners! Look at the plates! Brits! Poles! Mexicans!

Jean: Father…

(He hangs his head out of the window.)

Father: What the fuck are you at!

Jean: Father!

Father: Yes son.

Jean: I think perhaps I should leave home.

Father: Yes. Good idea.
By the way, I won't allow it.

Jean: Why?

Father: You have to stay and help me paint the estates. You have to stay and look after your sister.

Jean: I don't think it's good for me to look after Susan anymore.

Father: Well your mother can't do it. Your mother is too busy fucking every man in the county.

(Pause.)

Jean: What?

Father: Get out of the fucking way!
Look at these cars. Blacks everywhere. Who's running this fucking country?

Jean: What did you just say about mother?

Father: Identity, son. It's all about identity. Asians, blacks. You throw everyone in the mix like this, what happens to the Irish? What happens to us? What about the language? What about the music? The poets? These people don't care about that. They come over here and they bring their own identity with them. They build their own enclave. Why wouldn't they? No one wants to give up his own identity.
Better to help them sort out their problems in their own country than bring them all in here. It'll end in bloodshed. Mark my words. It'll end in fucking riots.

Jean: What did you say about mother?

Father: Not that I give a shit deep down. Right. We're on the M50. I'm having a snooze.

(He sleeps. Cuchulain stands outside Jean's window.)

Cuchulain: Leave them.

Jean: Why don't you leave me?

Cuchulain: Your sister will be leaving soon too.

Jean: Will she?

Cuchulain: The fairies will take her.

(Pause.)

Jean: Have I gone mad?

Cuchulain: No. But you will.

Jean: In that case, I'm taking control. I refuse to go mad. I refuse to acknowledge your presence.

(Pause. Jean sits, Cuchulain stands.)

Jean: For Christ's sake, go away.

Cuchulain: Not until you acknowledge your emptiness.

Jean: I will not. I'm living a good life. I'm helping my family make a living. I'm caring for my sister. I'm needed.

Cuchulain: You are being used, slave.

Jean: Then what? What do I do? Where do I go?

Cuchulain: To get what?

Jean: Contentment. Peace.

(The sound of car horns. Father suddenly wakes. Cuchulain exits.)

Father: The traffic's moving, Jean! Why didn't you wake me?

Jean: I'm sorry.

(He turns back to Cuchulain who has exited.)

Jean: Father, I don't think I'm very well.

Father: I don't think I am either. It's just the fumes. The pollution attacking the cells of your brain. You'll be alright once we're painting. The paint fumes will sort you out.

Jean: Father, do you need me?

Father: Yes… I just told you that. Why do you ask?

Jean: I don't know. Never mind.

Father: All right, I won't.

(A musical interlude as they arrive to their job, alight from their car, take the painting gear out of the boot, spread drop-cloths, set up trays, pour paint and begin to paint.)

Scene 9

***Sign: Holly Waits*.**

Jean and Father are painting.

Jean: Father. Why do I have a French name?

Father: Because your mother is an idiot. I wanted to call you Setanta.

Jean: You did?

Father: Yes. But your mother is so… continental. She thinks we're all the same. She doesn't get it.

Jean: Get what?

Father: Get that you're Irish. That's we're a race… not a breed.

(Pause.)

Jean: Is mother having an affair?

Father: Of course she is.

Jean: Did she tell you?

Father: No. I just know.

Jean: Why don't you do something?

Father: Like what?

Jean: I don't know. Anything? Don't you have any pride?

Father: Pride?

Shall I tell you about pride? I know more about watching paint dry, but I'll try to define it for you. Your mother hasn't loved me for a long time. I doubt if she ever really did. I don't think she even knows what love is. We were married and then she stopped… everything. She wouldn't even kiss me. You know, I used to write poetry. Yes, me, your stupid, manual-labouring father. She would read everything I read. Then we were married and it was as if it was all an act. She wanted children. She got them. But she didn't want that either. I don't think she knows what she wants.

I think it was many years ago that she started sleeping around. But I didn't. I had the opportunities. In fact, once I met a girl who loved me so much I thought my back would break with the heartache and I still restrained myself. She kissed me once. It was like living on the lip of a rose. The scent. I'll never forget it. She hated me for denying her. But I still held myself together. I maintained integrity. Not for your mother. For me… and for you.

Pride? Is that pride?

(Pause.)

Jean: I don't know.

Father: Neither do I. *(Pause.)* I try not to let my head fall. But I feel it falling.
I haven't taught you very well, have I?

Jean: No.

Father: It's hard to teach without answers.

(Pause. Father puts down his brush and aimlessly walks away leaving Jean alone.)

Jean: My father.

(Enter Holly.)

Holly: How old are you?

Jean: Who are you?

Holly: How old are you?

Jean: As old as the hills.

Holly: What are you doing?

Jean: Painting. What are you doing?

Holly: Bored.

Jean: Hmmm.

Holly: Tell me a story.

Jean: A story.

Holly: Yes. It's all that's left.

Jean: Okay. Once there was a girl with golden hair…

Holly: No. No. Tell me a story about you. Tell me something real.

Jean: I don't know if I should. Myths are better.

Holly: Why?

Jean: Because they're only stories. They can't hurt you. Real things can hurt. So I don't think I should tell you something real.

Holly: Why not? What's to lose?

Jean: I don't know you.

(Pause. Holly waits.)

Jean: Cuchulain comes to me and talks to me.

Holly: Really?

Jean: Yes.

Holly: What does he say to you?

Jean: He wants me to leave.

Holly: Where does he want you to go?

Jean: I don't know.
He never says.

Holly: What are you going to do?

Jean: I'm going to kill myself.

Holly: Really?

Jean: Yes.

Holly: How will you do that?

Jean: My Uncle has a pistol.

Holly: What kind of pistol?

Jean: 38.

Holly: Really?

Jean: No. I've never seen it. I presume it's a 38. Not too big, not too small. Something believable.

Holly: When will you kill yourself?

Jean: Tonight.

(Pause.)

Holly: Thank you.

Jean: For what?

Holly: For telling me something that's real.

(She sits.)

Holly: Do you mind if I stay and watch you paint?

Jean: I don't mind.

(Re-enter Father.)

Jean: Where did you go?

Father: To see if it was still there.

Jean: What?

Father: The bump. Who is she?

Jean: I don't know.

Holly: Holly.

Jean: Holly.

Father: Is she your girlfriend?

Jean: Yes.

Father: You can't bring your girlfriend to work.

Jean: Why not?

Father: The union says so. It's a rule.

Jean: Okay.

(No one moves. Father begins to paint again.)

Father: Holly, are you a Muslim?

Holly: Yes.

Father: Right then.

(They paint.)

Holly: No. I'm not really a Muslim.

Father: Oh. Right then.

(They paint.)

Holly: Are you a Muslim?

Father: No. I'm a disillusioned, dispossessed Irish Roman Catholic.

Holly: Hooray for that.

(They paint.)

Father: I like the gait of your stride, Holly. What are you doing with a bucket of dripping like Jean?

Holly: Finding life.

Father: You won't find any life in him.

Jean: Please don't call me a bucket of dripping in front of Holly.

Father: Spare me.

(He puts down his brush and walks away aimlessly.)

Jean: He has a problem with walking away. He just stops what he's doing and walks away aimlessly.

Holly: He could be insane.

Jean: Do you think?

Holly: Does he hallucinate like you?

Jean: I don't know… But my sister does. She sees fairies.

Holly: It could be a family condition. What about your mother?

Jean: I don't see her very much.

Holly: Did she leave your father?

Jean: No. She still lives with us. But she's not there very much.

Holly: My mother died in a collision with a car full of teenagers. She had her torso sliced in two by the dashboard.

(Pause.)

Jean: Did you cry?

Holly: No.
Yes.
Do you cry?

Jean: Only when I'm happy.

Holly: It's a strange

Jean: thing

Holly/Jean: to cry.

(Pause. Father enters wearing only his underpants.)

Jean: Father… What are you doing?

Father: Holly has inspired me to parade in my underwear. It is a rare day when a light comes into one's life and inspires one into his underwear.

Jean: But we're at work.

Father: If you can bring your girlfriend to work, I can wear my underwear. It is in the union contract.

Jean: Father, there is no union.

Father: Correct. That's the first time you have ever been correct. Holly, what do you think of my body?

Holly: I have no opinion.

Father: Do you think I'm sexy?

Holly: I resent being asked the question and so refuse to answer it.

Father: Shall I paint my body with this paint here?

Holly: I reserve the right to refuse to send this scenario in any direction. You must make your own choices and I will not get involved.

Father: Would you like me to put my clothes back on?

Holly: I reserve the right to refuse to send this scenario in any direction. You must make your own choices and I will not get involved.

Father: You're no fun.

(He exits.)

Jean: I'm sorry.

Holly: Why?

Jean: For my father. Perhaps you're right. Perhaps he has gone

Holly: insane

Jean: Or perhaps he's

Holly: ill.

Jean/Holly: I like you.

Holly: There's no need for you to be sorry. You're not your father. In fact you have no connection to him at all except that he's your father. And that's no connection to speak of.

Jean: But don't all men become like their fathers and all women like their mothers?

Holly: Yes, but they don't have too.

Jean: How does one avoid it?

Holly: By bathing regularly. How should I know?

(Pause.)

Jean: Thank you.

Holly: For what?

Jean: For separating me. I don't feel like killing me anymore.

Holly: But you must.

Jean: Why?

Holly: I think you know why. Don’t stop on my account.

Jean: Stop what?

Holly: Dying.

(Darkness.)

Holly: Keep dying.

Scene 10

Sign: The Doctor said….

Father sits opposite the Doctor for a very long moment.

Doctor: Is there anything you want to ask?

(Another very long moment.)

Doctor: Chemotherapy and then radio often solve this kind of thing.

(Another very long moment.)

Father: I'm going home now.

Doctor: Will we see you on Monday?

Father: I don't know.

(He stands to exit, but turns back.)

Father: Perhaps the bump will go away by itself.

Doctor: We refer to it as a lump. And no. It won't go away by itself.

(Father exits.)

ACT II
Scene 1

Sign: An Interlude with Annie Fanny

The home. Uncle. Father. Jean. Mother. Susan. They watch television.
Insurance salesperson knocks.

(A knock.)

Mother: Enter.

Jean: Whoever is at the door can't enter. It's locked and bolted three times.

Mother: Then open it, darling.

(Jean lets the insurance salesperson in.)

Sales: Hello.

Father: Hello. Who are you?

Sales: Your son invited me in. I am Annie Fanny. I sell insurance.

Father: What kind of insurance do you sell, Annie Fanny?

Annie: All kinds. What kind do you need?

Father: I have all kinds of insurance already. Health insurance, home insurance, car insurance, liability insurance, accidental death insurance, income protection insurance and probably many other insurances that I don't know I have.

Annie: Have you insured your liver?

(Pause.)

Father: I don't think so.

Annie: And the family? Are their livers insured?

Father: No.

Annie: Then you are at terrible risk and you are letting down your family by not ensuring that their livers are insured.

Father: How much is liver insurance?

Annie: A squillion Europes and seventy-five cents. But for you, I'll make a deal. If you insure your whole family including that strange man there, I'll make it three quarters of a squillion squids and seventy-eight spents.

Mother: But will you dance for us?

Annie: Dance for you?

Mother: Yes. We have 467 channels on our television and we can't find anything to watch. It's getting late and soon the pornography will come. But until then, we are lost. We require entertainment. Entertainment with gay abandon.

Annie: But I sell insurance. I don't know how to dance.

Mother: Not even a military two-step?
Jean, do a military two-step with Miss Fanny.

Jean: I don't know how to two-step, mother.

Mother: You useless fuck.
We all know the Pride of Erin. Let us dance the Pride of Erin.

Uncle: None of us know the Pride of Erin, you fucking psychopath.

Mother: That'll be enough of your lip, brother, or I'll tell the tale.

Uncle: Sorry.

Mother: You don't want me to tell the tale, do you?

Uncle: Please… please… no. Don't tell. I beg you.

Mother: Pull yourself together.

Uncle: Very well.

Mother: Listen, Miss Fanny. My husband paints houses. Do you know how many houses are being built at the moment? Shitloads. Shitloads of half-built, half-finished shacks in estates that will one day be ghettos of gangland criminality. He paints them. He makes them look beautiful. You make a fortune by insuring them for outrageous sums that they are simply not worth. They will fall down, mark my words.

But my point in ranting in this most impolite manner, provoking all and sundry with my opinionated opinions, is that my husband has more money than you could poke your Fanny at. So he can buy your insurance. All you have to do is dance.

Annie: But I don't know how to dance.

Mother: What about a magic trick? Do a trick.

Annie: I'm not a magician.

Mother: What about a poem. Recite a poem.

Annie: I really don't know any…

Mother: But we are a nation of poets.

Annie: I don't know any poems.

Mother: Then sing a fucking song.

Annie: I don't know any…

Susan: Come all you loyal heroes…
(She sings The Rocks of Bawn in its entirety.)

Annie: Well. I suppose I should be going then.

Father: No sale tonight, Miss Fanny.

Annie: Yes… yes. No sale.

Father: Do you insure the pancreas?

Annie: I do!

Father: Will you insure a pancreas if you know it is plagued with cancer?

(She backs away and then exits quickly.)

(Pause.)

(She returns.)

Annie: Ummm. Sorry. The door is locked. Does it require a key?

Jean: Oh yes… My fault.

(Jean exits with Annie and we hear the door open and then slam closed. Jean returns.)

Jean: I think I'll go to bed.

Father: Leave yourself alone. You'll go blind.

Jean: Father. That's not true. That's an old wives tale.

Father: Eat my shit.

Jean: Father, is your pancreas really plagued with cancer?

Father: Riddled.

Uncle: You wouldn't really tell them the tale, would you?

Mother: Don't bet on it.

Uncle: I'll be good. I promise.

Mother: Shut up.

Jean: Mother, are you having an affair?

Mother: Shut up.

(Cuchulain enters and signals Jean to follow him. Jean exits after Cuchulain.)

Mother: He's beginning to behave like you. He wanders.

Father: I think I'll have a drink.

Uncle: Of alcohol?

Father: Yes.

Mother: Over my dead body you will.

Father: And a fag. I think I'll smoke a fag.

Mother: Not in this day and age.

Father: It might relax me.

Mother: And help you forget your lot? Too bad. Deal with your lot. Suck it up and deal with it. There is a smoking and alcohol ban in this house.

Father: Deal with the fact that you're cheating on me? Is that what you mean?

Uncle: *(Rising.)* Are you accusing my sister of being a slut?

Father: Sit down, you troglodyte.

Mother: I'll deal with my lot and you deal with yours.

Father: What if I put a stop to your little affair.

Mother: How, may I ask, do you intend to do that?

Father: By imposing my will. By putting my foot down. By standing up like a man and refusing to be humiliated further.

Mother: Listen to me, Bill. Listen very very carefully. You have no power over me.

Father: I don't want power over you.

Mother: You have no power over me.

Father: You're not listening. I don't want power over you. All I want is for you to stop humiliating me by sleeping…

Mother: *(Interrupting him.)* You have no power over me.

(She exits. Pause.)

Father: Did you talk to Jean?

Uncle: Yes.

Father: What did you want to talk to him about?

Uncle: Death.

Father: Is that so?

Uncle: It is so.

Father: Tell me what exactly about death.

Uncle: Why should I?

Father: Because if you don't I'll attack you violently.

Uncle: Very well. I have been envenoming spiders. Over the past months or more, I have developed a spider that can kill. An Irish, killer spider.

Father: Why would you want to do that?

Uncle: I don't know.

Anyway, I first developed a venom that could cripple. Then I developed a venom that could kill in several hours. Then I developed a venom that can kill instantly. Now I have developed a venom that is so toxic, it can kill before death knows it is death.

Father: Why don't you go and get a job?

Uncle: Work is for slaves.

Father: Is that a personal sleight?

Uncle: Not really. But you are a slave. And I am not.

Father: You live under this roof, playing with your fucking experiments. You eat my food, sleep here in the attic room free of board and you have the gall to sit there and call me a slave.

Uncle: Everyone's a slave.

Father: You're a fucking slave.

Uncle: No. I am not a slave. You grind. You slave and grind. Like two horrible shards of slate grinding together. You are a grinder.

Father: So that I can have money.

Uncle: Money. Humph.

Father: What if I threw you out on the street?

Uncle: You wouldn't. My sister wouldn't allow it.

(Pause.)

Father: Do you have any idea how much I hate you?

Uncle: I can guess.

Father: Mark my words, you perverted priest. I will slay you.

Uncle: Consider them marked.

Scene 2

Jean searches through his Uncle's room. Cuchulain watches. He can't find the gun. Eventually he spots the spider in its jar. He goes to it, picks it up. Looks at it. He opens the jar and puts his hand in. He is bitten and recoils with the pain. He does not fall or die. He looks at the bite mark and suddenly drops the jar. It smashes. The spider escapes. He attempts to recapture it, but is gone. He takes a pan and brush and cleans up the glass. Darkness.

Scene 3

The Fairies flit about Susan who sits in the living room alone eating crisps.

Sign: With a Faerie…

Fairy 1: Come now. No more crisps.

Fairy 2: No more.

Susan: I like crisps.

Fairy 1: You are being poisoned by them.

Susan: I don't feel poisoned.

Fairy 2: You are full of poison. The air. The water. It is all poisoned. It is all contaminated.

Fairy 2: All things are finished, Susan. There is nothing left to be gleaned. There is nothing else except death.
Death.

Susan: I want to see the death.

Fairy 1: Why? Why wait to witness it. It is carnage. It is a nightmare. Radiation.

Fairy 2: Bacterial nightmares. Infection and suffering.

Susan: Let me see it. I want to see it.

Fairy 1: Can't you smell it?

Susan: I have a cold.

Fairy 2: Then wait and see it if you must.

(They fly away.)

Susan: I am new.

Scene 4

Breakfast. Jean enters and sits at the table.

Jean: Good Morning.

Mother: Indeed.

Susan: My Weetabix has a funny smell.

Mother: Then don't pour your father's paint on it. Use the milk.

Susan: Yes. But the paint is prettier.

Mother: One is not prettier than the other. They are both white. Just plain white.

Father: White.

(Pause.)

Jean: I don't think I'll be having breakfast this morning.

Uncle: Why not? Are you on a hunger strike?

Jean: No. Nothing like that. I have no appetite.

Father: No appetite. People starved to death in those very fields out there one hundred and fifty years ago and he has no appetite. What a muddle-headed dimension.

Mother: If he's not hungry he's not hungry. Give yours to your sister. She's ruined hers with paint.

Susan: I've already eaten it.

Jean: I'm going to have a bath.

Father: At 7:30 in the morning? What a muddle-headed dimension.

Mother: Take your sister. She has paint all over her. You can both fit.

Jean: Mother. I can't fit in the bath with Susan. She's too big.

Mother: She's a whippet.

Jean: Mother. She is enormous. And besides, I don't want to bath with her. I don't want to bath her. She's a woman now. It's not nice to bath your sister when she's a woman.

Mother: Your father can't do it. He'll let her drown.

Jean: What about you? Can you do it?

Mother: I don't have time. I have a meeting.

Father: Give up the charade.

Jean: Can't Uncle do it?

Uncle: Yes. Yes… Let me do it.

Mother: Not a chance.

Uncle: Oh.

Mother: She's your responsibility, Jean. And clean her teeth.

Jean: Why? They'll be whiter this way.

Mother: Don't be smart.

(Pause.)

Jean: Come on, Susan.

(Jean takes Susan and goes downstage to an isolated area and helps her take off her clothes. The fairies are in the bathroom.)

Susan: Don't you like to look at me?

Jean: It's not that.

Susan: It is. I'm very ugly. The fairies say I eat too many crisps.

Fairy 1: You do, Susan.

Fairy 2: Look at you. Crisps are just pure fat and oil.

Jean: It's your condition, Susan. It's to do with your glands. Don't listen to the fairies. You eat all the crisps you want.

Susan: But I wouldn't be as ugly if I wasn't fat.

Fairy 1: Forget about that. It's the sheer disgustingness of crisps. It's the contamination of it all. It's the litter in the river.

Jean: You're not ugly.

Susan: Yes I am. You'd like to bath me more if I was prettier.

Jean: No, I wouldn't. I'm your brother so I wouldn't like it either way. It's just something I have to do because the doctor says you can't do it by yourself.

Susan: The fairies say death is coming.

Fairy 2: If you keep eating those fucking crisps it'll be sooner than later.

Jean: You're not going to die.

Susan: I wasn't meant to live till now. Fourteen they said. That was long ago.

Jean: Doctors can be wrong.

Susan: The fairies know it will be soon. They want me to go away with them to the Boyne.

Jean: The Boyne? Did they say that?

Susan: Yeah.

Jean: Susan, do you know what the Boyne is?

Susan: Yeah.

Jean: What is it?

Susan: It's a place with water and green valleys. It's paradise.

Jean: It's not paradise. It's a river.

Susan: It's where the dark green and light green are. And the fairies live there and fly across the water. The swans are there. And there's a really smart fish.

Jean: A smart fish. A salmon?

Susan: Yeah. A smart fish. If you eat it you'll get to be clever. If I ate it, it would stop me being stupid.

Jean: You're not stupid.

Susan: You're stupid.

Jean: No, I'm not.

Susan: You are stupid.

Jean: Not as stupid as you. Clean your teeth before the paint dries on them.

Susan: I feel sick from the paint.

Jean: In your tummy?

Susan: Yeah.

Jean: Do you want to throw up?

Susan: Yeah.

Jean: Then go into the toilet. Go, go…

(He pushes her off left. Pause. He looks in the mirror.)

Jean: I've died.

(Cuchulain stands beside him.)

Cuchulain: I told you this would happen.

Jean: I'm still breathing. Why am I still moving?

Cuchulain: I don't know. Sometimes people die and stay on.

Jean: Am I a ghost?

Cuchulain: I don't know. How do you feel?

(Pause.)

Jean: Better.

Cuchulain: Yes. Your head is up. You haven't let your head fall.

(The sound of Susan vomiting.)

Cuchulain: Jesus.

Jean: You can stay and help me with her.

(Cuchulain exits quickly. The sound of Susan vomiting. Jean exits after her.)

Father: Where are you going today?

Mother: Out.

Father: Yes, but where?

Mother: You know I'm not going to answer you, so why do you bother?

Father: I'm asking you not to go.

Mother: That won't work either.

Father: I'm not telling you. I'm asking you. From my heart.

Mother: You have no heart.

(She exits. Sound of Susan vomiting.)

Father: *(Alone. He stares around him as if in a daze for a long moment. He stares at the audience. He moves towards them, looks at them as if they are animals in a zoo, exhibits in a gallery.)*
There it is.
(Eventually Darkness.)

Scene 5

At work.

Father: We are to be paid today. Great sums of money.

Jean: Great.

Father: Mr Mcmanus will come by with money. He will give me a cheque worth great sums of money and I will pass on a small percentage of it to you and call it your wage. Then it will be taxed. And you will be rich.

(Jean is silent.)

Father: Does this filthy richness not give you an erection?

Jean: No.

Father: Spoilt. You didn't have to work during the eighties. You'd be jumping up and down about this richness if you'd had to work during the eighties. People struggled then.

Jean: What is struggle like?

Father: It's a burden. It makes life a shit-filled misery.

Jean: Really?

Father: Yes really. What do you mean really?

Jean: I don't know. I don't… I don't want to seem ungrateful… but if you struggled, you wouldn't worry so much about wanking. You'd be too busy finding your next meal.

Father: That's probably true. You're coming up with more truisms all the time.

Jean: And if there was a war… you'd have something to fight for. You'd have a direction. A purpose.

Father: Can't you be a man without a war?

Jean: I don't know. Can you?

(Pause.)

Father: I don't understand the question.

Jean: But you asked it?

(Father exits, walking aimlessly away. Holly enters.)

Holly: Damn.

Jean: Why do you say damn?

Holly: You said you were going to kill yourself. And you haven't. How disappointing.

Jean: But I have.

Holly: You're just like all the others. Tell you they're going to do something exciting to try to get into your pants and then chicken out.

Jean: I didn't try to get into your pants.

Holly: Don't you want to get into my pants?

Jean: No.

Holly: Don't lie. All the boys want to get into my pants.

Jean: Well I don't.

Holly: You're such a fucking liar. You're like the rest. Ruled by your dick.

Jean: No. I'm serious. I have no desire to get into your pants… I have no… desire.

(Pause.)

Holly: So if I took you into that spare room and locked the door and took off my clothes and spread my legs, you wouldn't shag me?

Jean: That's right. *(He continues painting.)*

(Pause.)

Holly: Come on then, let's go. I don't believe you. I have to see this for myself.

Jean: Go yourself. I don't want to.

Holly: This is fucking insane! You're a boy and I'm offering you my body…

Jean: Keep it.

(Pause.)

Holly: Okay, you got me interested again. What's the story?

Jean: Like I told you. I committed suicide last night.

Holly: You paint a good wall for a dead man.

Jean: I guess.

Holly: Show me the bullet holes.

Jean: No. I didn't use a gun. I got bitten by a spider.

Holly: There's no poisonous spiders in Ireland, you halfwit.

Jean: Yes there is. My Uncle has genetically engineered one. It kills so fast that death doesn't even have time to realize that it is death. That's why I'm still moving and walking around and painting walls and shit.

Holly: Is your uncle a fucking idiot?

Jean: Yes.

Holly: Then my assessment of the situation is that you're not dead. The spider isn't poisonous.

Jean: Feel my pulse.

(He puts out his arm. Holly pauses, wary for a moment. Then she feels his wrist.)

Holly: *(Pulling away.)* Jesus Christ.

Jean: And I don't have to breathe. I can hold my breath as long as I want. I only have to inhale to speak.

Holly: Fucking hell.

Jean: Yeah. Pretty cool.

Holly: What will happen to you?

Jean: I don't know.

(Father enters followed by Mr McManus.)

Father: Jean, this is Mr McManus.

Jean: I know. We've met.

McManus: Hello Jean. That's a fine bit of painting you're doing there.

Jean: Thank you.

McManus: I see you've met my daughter. Holly, you didn't offer this boy your body, did you?

Holly: Yeah. But he wasn't interested.

McManus: What's wrong with my daughter's body, son?

Jean: Nothing, sir… It's a fine body.

McManus: Then why don't you want to shag it?

Jean: I'm… just not feeling myself… today.

McManus: Well, what's wrong with you, boy?

Jean: I… just feel more like talking… or something.

McManus: Talking. Bill, let it be known your son is gay. Generation of faggots. That's the problem, isn't it Bill?

Father: Yes, you're on the money there, Mr McManus.

McManus: Speaking of money, I have a large sum for you but thought I'd run a suggestion by you before I give it to you.

I'm building two more estates as you know.

Father: Yes… We'd be happy to paint them.

McManus: Well, you see, in our booming Celtic economy, there's a little bug called competition that sneaks in, Bill. There's a lot of painters wanting those jobs now. Well there's one other painter that wants that job. Lithuanian guy. Can't pronounce his name.

But look, I'm happy to give it to you… let's say in exchange for twenty-percent of this cheque I'm about to give you.

(Pause.)

Father: Well, Mr McManus, sir. We earned that money and we've done a good job here for you. You know we'd do a good job on the other est….

McManus: Now, Bill, let's not get into the bleeding heart of the thing. We both know how this works. You send me a text message before five and let me know which way you'd like to go.
Holly, you keep your fucking pants on, for Christ's sake.

Holly: Yes Daddy.

(Mr McManus exits. Pause.)

Jean: Father, are you alright?

(Father walks away aimlessly.)

Holly: What does he expect? You should see the brown paper envelopes that my Dad brings to work every day. Planning Permission for this, license for that. You pay up or wait two months and by then someone's got in ahead of you. Can't be helped.

Jean: It's crooked.

Holly: No it isn't. It's life.

Jean: No it isn't. It's crooked.

Holly: It's a crooked life. Twisted.
Sure you're not interested in that shag?

Jean: You want to have sex with a man whose heart isn't beating?

Holly: My mother did.

Jean: I don't think I could get an erection if I wanted to and I don't want to.

Holly: Okay. Can I watch you paint?

Jean: If you like.

(Pause. Jean paints. Father reenters.)

Father: Fight! We must fight this injustice!

Jean: Fight?

Father: Fight! Now you have your war, Setanta.

Jean: My name is Jean.

Father: We have to engage this new enemy. Bloody corruption. Poisoned, bloody corruption eating us from the inside out. We must expose the cancer within and attack it with various forms of radiation.

Jean: Father…

Father: No more, I say! No more! This is MY island and I won't see it run by a shower of cowboys.

Jean: Father…

Father: That spineless worm, trying to grub me out of my hard earned money. Threatening to take the work I've earned and proven myself worthy of with my own two hands and the slavery of my very own child! Damn him to hell!

Jean: Father, Holly is still here.

Father: Oh. You won't say anything to your Daddy, will you hon?

Holly: Maybe.

Father: Here... *(he reaches into his pocket).* Will fifty cover it?

Holly: Okay. *(She takes the fifty and skips away.)*

Father: Now. To action, Setanta. I'll go to the union. You go to the Ombudsman. If that doesn't work, we'll go to the police and file a complaint of extortion and bribery.

(Pause.)

Jean: Should we finish this house first?

Father: Of course. Now paint! Paint like there's no tomorrow!

Scene 6

Mother and Lover. They sip coffee.

Lover: What's the matter?

Mother: Nothing.

Lover: Feeling guilty?

Mother: I beg your pardon?

Lover: Are you feeling guilty? Your husband knows, doesn't he?

Mother: Of course he knows. How could he not know? He knows me better than I know myself.

Lover: So you're feeling guilty.

Mother: I don't feel guilt.

Lover: I think you do.

Mother: Very sure of yourself all of a sudden, aren't you?

Lover: Maybe.

Mother: What if I walked out of here and never came back?

Lover: You wouldn't do that. You need me as much as I need you.

Mother: You're wrong. I don't need anyone.

Lover: Of course you do. Everyone needs someone.

Mother: I don't.

Lover: No. You're surrounded by people and you pretend you don't need them, but you can't walk away from them. No matter how hard you try, you can't walk away. You can't leave your husband and you can't leave me. You're trapped. You're a slave. You can't cut yourself free.

Mother: Watch me.

(She exits. He puts on his jacket and goes downstage to a seat.)

Scene 7

Susan sits in the sitting room. The Fairies are with her.

Fairy 1: We can't hang around waiting for you any more, Susan. This place is not good for us. It makes us ill.

Fairy 2: Please come now.

Susan: Soon. I'll come soon. Don't be so impatient.

Fairy 1: Then what's there to wait for?

Susan: Jean.

Fairy 2: He can't help you now. He can't come with you.

Susan: Yes he can. He will come to the Boyne and we'll live there forever because he loves me.

Fairy 1: He loves you?

Susan: He loves me very much.

Fairy 2: Did he say so?

Susan: He doesn't have to say it.
I'm going to wait for him. Wait till he's ready to come.

Fairy 1: Fine.

Fairy 2: The weird priest approaches. Let us away.

(The fairies fly away.)

Uncle: Fuck! Fucking fuck!

Susan: Why are you using bad words?

Uncle: Because the spider is gone. My precious baby is gone!

Susan: Spider? What spider?

Uncle: The spider! My poisonous, precious baby! The beginning of the end!

Susan: There are no poisonous spiders in Ireland.

Uncle: Shut up.

Susan: It might be in the house somewhere.

Uncle: No. It's in a jar. The jar and all is gone. It was him.

Susan: Who?

Uncle: Your father. He's trying to kill me. He thinks he can kill me with my own spider.

Susan: My father isn't the killing type.

Uncle: In case you haven't noticed yet, you are retarded and stupid.

Susan: I'm not retarded. I'm autistic.

Uncle: You are retarded. There's a tumor on your brain.

Susan: A tumor? What does a tumor mean?

Uncle: It means you're out of luck.
Now take off your clothes.

Susan: Daddy said I shouldn't.

Uncle: You're stupid. Take off your clothes. Do as you're told.

(She begins to undress. Darkness. The Fairies appear.)

Fairy 1: Such sadness.

Fairy 2: The horror.

Fairy 1: Made in the image of the thief. He steals that which he can only get by deception.

Fairy 2: Now the illness is manifest. Now it becomes a real plague.

Fairy 1: A society diseased. A plague that must change everything forever. So that touch becomes poison.

Fairy 2: Affection becomes forbidden.

Fairy 1: And the hugless society breeds its robots.

Fairy 2: The skin starves and dries.

Fairy 1: And desolation for all. Barren fields. Blasted heaths.

Fairy 2: Horror.

Fairy 1: And desolation.

Scene 8

Lover sits and Father sits opposite him.

Father: So I need help. I'm being conned. Extorted. I've been union thirty years. I've paid all my fees. I've never asked for help. I need help now.

Lover: You're Bill.

Father: Yes.

Lover: I'm afraid we can't help you. You see, the Lithuanian gentleman is also a union member.

Father: But… I'm being blackmailed. I'm being blackmailed for my next contract… Can't you understand?

Lover: I'm afraid it's common practice… Bill. It's just a flow of funds. Think about it. If you pay the money and get the contract you will continue to earn great ass loads of money. You will make back the payment in no time.

Father: But it isn't fair.

Lover: And nor would it be fair to the Lithuanian gentleman if we were to represent you to ensure you get a contract that he is also a tender for. Now that wouldn't be fair, would it?

Father: But… thirty years I've been a member… right through the eighties! The eighties when there was no work… I still paid my fees. I didn't miss a payment. It's blackmail. It's illegal.

Lover: I'm afraid it's common practice in my day and age. It all started with Charlie Haughey. He was the catalyst. He gave us all permission.

Father: My day and age? This is MY day and age. I'm still here! I'm still alive, am I not?

Lover: Of course… Bill. I'm afraid it's a matter of adjusting to the modern format.

Father: But it's illegal. Haughey was a criminal. He committed criminal offenses.

Lover: It depends which way you look at it.

Father: There is only one way to look at it.

Lover: I'm afraid there's many ways to look at things. Let me tell you a story. My great great grandfather was a landlord during the famine.

Father: That explains a thing or two.

Lover: No. You don't understand. He became a pauper by keeping his tenants and making sure they didn't starve. He spent his last shillings getting them safely off to America.

(Pause.)

Father: Is that true?

Lover: I'm afraid I don't know.

Father: Then why bother telling me that?

Lover: What if it is true? I'm afraid the truth is a little more illusive than we give it credit for.

Father: Are you?

Lover: I beg your pardon?

Father: Are you afraid?

Lover: I'm afraid I don't know what you mean?

Father: You've said many times that you're afraid.

Lover: I have? Well I'm not.

Father: Shall I make you afraid?

Lover: Is that a threat… Bill?

(Pause.)

Father: Do you know what struggle is?

Lover: Struggle?

Father: As in the eighties… struggle.

Lover: I wasn't even a teenager in the eighties, I'm afraid.

Father: No. Of course.
Thankyou for your time.

Lover: Sure.

Scene 9

Jean and the Ombudsman's assistant.

Jean: Hello. I'd like an appointment with the Ombudsman.

Assistant: Just a moment.

(She flicks the pages of a magazine. A long pause.)

Jean: I'd like to see the Ombudsman today if at all possible. It's a matter of some urgency.

(The assistant ignores Jean.)

Jean: Excuse me.

Assistant: What?

Jean: What do you mean what? I'd like to see the Ombudsman.

Assistant: That's not possible. The Ombudsman is very busy.

Jean: Yes, but this is a matter of the utmost urgency.

Assistant: I'm sure it is.

Jean: It is. It is a legal matter. It is about exposing an insidious corruption.

Assistant: Yes. I'm sure. Is it for the greater good?

Jean: I'm sorry?

Assistant: Is it for the greater good or are you only interested in resolving a personal matter for your own personal or financial satisfaction.

Jean: I'm not sure if I know what you mean.

Assistant: Well, I had a fella in here this morning who was bound and determined to complain that only four trains a day go to his town so he can't get home from work unless he drives. He misses the last train you see because he works until twenty after six. He came in here bulling on about the public transport system being inadequate, but really he was only interested in improving his own lifestyle. He just wanted a train for himself, or preferably a few trains so he could go and drink alcohol after work and then choose which train he felt like getting home on. It was an entirely selfish complaint.

Jean: But surely it would be so much better if he could take his car off the road for five days of the week. Better for traffic and the air. And stop him being tempted to drink and drive. And perhaps a number of other people would be able to do the same.

Assistant: Are you a communist?

Jean: I don't think so.

Assistant: That sounds like something a communist would say.

Jean: Does it?

Assistant: I suppose you want free health and education.

Jean: If I pay tax, yes.

Assistant: I knew it. A communist. Are you a Marxist or a Leninist?

Please don't tell me you're a Stalinist.

Jean: I'm neither. I'm an Irishman.

Assistant: With a name like Jean? Sounds French to me.

Jean: It's only a name.

Assistant: Then your parents must be communists. French communist revolutionary agitators planted here to undermine the fabric of Irish society.

Jean: What are you talking about?

Assistant: Are you a Muslim?

Jean: No, for Christ's sake.
I think we're getting off the topic.

Assistant: Oh, are we?

Jean: I believe so.

Assistant: You're right, we are. Are you a Marxist or a Leninist or a Stalinist.

Jean: That wasn't the topic either. Wind back.

Assistant: Oh yes. You can't have another train to get your drunken ass home from work. You'll just have to join all the other slaves in their cars and wheel it.

Jean: No. That wasn't me. That wasn't my complaint.

Assistant: It wasn't? Oh yes. Is it personal or for the greater good.

Jean: Which one would help me in my efforts to see a result?

Assistant: Probably neither.

Jean: My father is being blackmailed by a contractor. He is being extorted out of twenty percent of his earnings.

Assistant: *(Suddenly extremely concerned.)* What? Oh my God! I'll... I'll... Oh goodness, what will I do! Wait a moment... I'll make an appointment immediately… I'll put you up the schedule to first priority. That's what I'll do.

Jean: Well, that would be most helpful.

Assistant: In fact, don't move a muscle. I'll see if he's in now.

Jean: Oh… Very well then.

(The assistant leaps to her feet and exits. Jean waits. Pause. He continues to wait. This should be done in real time. He waits several minutes and the assistant does not return.)

Jean: Hello? Hello?

(Pause.)

Jean: Hello?

(Pause. He knocks on the desk. Pause.)

Jean: Hello?

(He eventually exits. Pause. The assistant returns, sits and continues to read her magazine. Darkness.)

Scene 10

Pub. Jean, Father and Bartender.

Jean: I have to take a piss.

Father: Once you do you'll be up and down like a yo yo.

Jean: Why?

Father: It's the drink. Once you take the first piss, you're at it for the night.

Jean: Okay.

Bartender: He's right. It's a dreadful poison I'm feeding you.

Jean: Okay.

(Jean goes.)

Father: Shall I have another?

(Bartender slams a whisky on the bar almost before he has finished his sentence.)

Father: The travelers are gone.

Bartender: That's why they call them travelers.

(Pause.)

Father: Must be some life. Moving all the time.

Bartender: Must be something to be able to get up and leave everything behind you. Just move on.

Father: Must be something. Must make you feel very free.

Bartender: Must do.

Father: But the poverty. Living by the skin of your teeth. Don't know if I'd like that.

Bartender: How much does freedom cost?

(Pause. Suddenly they reach for each other across the bar and kiss passionately. They break.)

Father: I said I'd never do that again.

Bartender: Why?

Father: Because I made a promise.

Bartender: So did she.

Father: That doesn't matter.

Bartender: Yes it does.

Father: I made a promise. It's all I have. It's the one solid decision I made that I won't break. It's my rock.

Bartender: It's shattered.

Father: No.

Bartender: It's destroyed.

Father: Stop.

(He cries. Pause.)

Father: It's going to end soon.

Bartender: What is?

(Jean re enters. Father hides his tears.)

Jean: Maybe I'll have another anyway.

Bartender: Sure, kid.
(She serves him.)
Do you have a girlfriend, Jean?

Jean: Yep.

Bartender: Doesn't surprise me.
Your father was a lady killer once.

Jean: Was he?

Bartender: Once.

Jean: Who did he kill?

Bartender: Lots of girls.

Jean: Well, I'm sure he didn't mean it.

Bartender: No. He didn't mean it. He was of the old school.

Jean: What does that mean?

Bartender: It means he believed.

Father: Stop talking now.

(Pause)

Jean: I think I'm drunk.

Father: That's good. Enjoy it.

Jean: I think I want to sing a song.

Father: Do then.

(Jean sings the beginning of "Wake me up Before you Go-Go" by Wham. Father stops him.)

Father: Perhaps we'll drink.

Jean: Very well.

Father: Don't you know anything traditional?

Jean: You never taught me.
You taught Susan.

Father: That was a long time ago.

Jean: She remembers.

Father: She has a vast mindscape.

Jean: Yes. *(Pause.)* Will she die?

Father: The doctors said it would be years ago. She keeps going.

Jean: Do you want her to die?

(Pause.)

Father: She doesn't belong. She's pure. She should go.

Jean: Go where?

Father: Where we're all going.

Jean: Where are we going?

Father: A good question, Jean.

Scene 11

Father in Uncle's room. He appears to be conducting an experiment, brandishing a long syringe of some brightly coloured liquid. He injects it into a spider, then carefully places the spider in a jar which he hides.

ACT III
Scene 1

The living room.

Father: Fuck.

Jean: What?

Father: No response from the Ombudsman's office?

Jean: No. It's been three weeks. They said they'd make us first priority, but I don't think they were being serious.

Father: What's that God awful smell? Jean. It's you. You smell. It's been getting worse and worse. You are avoiding bathing so that you don't have to wash your sister. It's disgusting. Go and have a bath and take your sister with you. I washed her three days ago. She's ready for another bath.

Jean: You sprayed her with the garden hose, father. That's not washing. And it could give her a cold.

Father: It's more washing than you've been doing.

Jean: I have been washing. I don't know why I smell. I don't understand it.

Father: Well go and wash again and take your sister with you.

Jean: I don't want to.

Father: *(Suddenly exploding.)* No one wants to do anything! But you have to fucking do it! It's the way of the world! It's the fault of Adam and Eve. It's hell! Hell I tell you, but it's the fucking world. So do it NOW!

(Stunned pause. Susan begins to cry. Jean takes her to the bathroom downstage.)

Mother: What's up your ass?

Father: What do you think's up my ass? I've been fucked out of my job. My son stinks, my daughter's fucked in the head and my wife's a fucking prostitute. *(Looks at the Uncle.)* I don't know what the fuck you are.
(Quietly.) All my dignity is gone. Every last shred of my manhood has been taken from me and flushed down the fucking toilet.

Mother: Why don't you kill yourself?

Father: You wouldn't want that.

Mother: Wouldn't I?

Father: Life insurance doesn't cover for suicide.

Mother: Then smash your car into a tree. Make it look like an accident. Everyone's doing it.

Father: Do you remember our wedding day?

Mother: Stop it.

Father: I was still drunk from the night before.

Mother: I don't remember.

Father: And you were wearing that chiffon thing, with no back.

Mother: Shut up.

Father: Who's your lover?

(Pause.)

Father: Tell me. Who is he? There's no point in my trying to stop this hurricane, so just tell me. What difference does it make to you?

Mother: *(A pause.)* He's young.

Father: How old?

Mother: Twenty-two.

Father: Is he handsome?

Mother: He's a man.

Father: I'd like to meet him.

Mother: Don't be absurd.

Father: Why not? I'm not going to stop you having an affair with him…

Mother: You can't stop…

Father: Can't… I can't stop you. But you're going to go on living under my roof so I might as well just get past it and meet him. Then you can see him here and we can get on with our lives.

(Pause.)

Mother: Are you serious?

Father: Yes. What's the point of all this intrigue and bitterness? I can't stand it anymore. Let's have it out in the open and get on with it.

Mother: You'd do that?

Father: What did I say to you that day?

Mother: What day?

Father: You don't remember. On our wedding day. I came to you before… in the morning. I wasn't supposed to. Maybe I cursed the day. And I said, forget the vows. All I want is to make you happy. I'll do everything I can. That's my vow.
If this will make you happy, then…

(Pause.)

Mother: I'll consider.

Father: Do.

(Downstage. Susan has undressed and gotten into the bath. The Fairies have appeared. Jean takes off his shirt to reveal cystic wounds covering his torso.)

Susan: What are those?

Jean: Sores.

Susan: Why have you got sores?

Jean: I'm not sure why.

Susan: Do you have AIDS?

Jean: I don't think so. I'm a virgin and I don't take drugs, so I can't see how.

Susan: It said in a movie that AIDS gives you sores.

Jean: Then it's probably true.

(Pause. Jean touches one of the sores.)

Susan: Do they hurt?

Jean: No.

Susan: They're smelly.

Jean: Are they? I can't smell them.

Susan: They're really smelly. Like Felix.

Jean: Like Felix the cat… when he died?

Susan: Like Felix in the attic.

Jean: That's right.

Susan: Is it death?

Jean: I think it might be.

Susan: The fairies said there would be death. And they said it would be smelly.

Jean: I thought they were talking about you dying.

Susan: Must have been talking about you.

Fairy 1: *(Weakly)* It is death for all. Desolation. So sick.

Fairy 2: Please Susan. Let us go now.

Fairy 1: The weird priest cometh.

(The Uncle has made his way downstage.)

Uncle: Do you want help with Susan in the bath?

Jean: No, Uncle. Go away. You know you're not allowed.

Uncle: What are those things on your body?

Jean: Sores. I was bitten by your spider.

Uncle: You fucker! It was you! You stole her! Where is she?

Jean: I don't know. It escaped.

Susan: You got bitten by a spider?

Jean: Three weeks ago.

Uncle: *(Studying the sores. Feeling Jean's neck for a pulse.)* It's true. It kills before death knows it is death. Death is only realizing it is meant to be doing its job now, three weeks after the bite. Incredible.

Susan: Are you going to die, Jean?

Jean: I'm already dead, Susie.
How long will it take to kill me?

Uncle: It already has killed you, stupid goat. You're decomposing. Though you are animate. I don't know. I've never seen anything like it.

Jean: What will happen to me?

Uncle: If it is decomposition as we know it, you will slowly fall to pieces. Limbs will drop off, skin will melt away. Bacteria is eating you from those sores. The bacteria will slowly eat you up. You will decay.

Jean: And I'll feel no pain.

Susan: No pain.

Uncle: I don't know. You're the first to be bitten.
What happened to the spider?

Jean: It fell out of my hands. The jar smashed. I tried to catch it but it ran away.

Uncle: God, it could be anywhere!

(Pause.)

Uncle: Why don't you go and rest. I'll bath Susan.

Jean: Why don't you fuck off?

Uncle: Fine.

(He goes.)

Susan: Are you dying Jean?

Jean: I'm already dead.

Susan: Can I die too?

Jean: You will one day. Everyone does in the end.

Susan: But can I die and stay around like you?

Jean: No. I don't think so. Now come on, wash yourself. I know you know how.

Susan: I want you to do it.

Jean: Please Susan. You know I don't like to. You're twenty-one years old. You can do it yourself.

Susan: But it's nice when you do it. It makes me feel nice. And Uncle made my skin feel all crawly.

Jean: Did he touch you? You know you're not to let him.

Susan: He said I had to do as I was told.

(A pause. Jean roars like a lion. The others in the living room hear and turn their heads to the sound.)

Susan: I'm scared when you roar.

Jean: I'm sorry.
(Pause.)
I felt… I felt that.

Susan: Can you wash me? It feels nice when you wash me.

Jean: I'm sure it does, but that's not normal. I'm your brother. You shouldn't feel nice when I do it.

Susan: But no one else holds me.

(Pause.)

Jean: What?

Susan: Mammy and Daddy don't touch me anymore.

Jean: They don't hold you? They don't touch you? At all?

Susan: No. Do they touch you?

Jean: No… but I don't need to be.

Susan: They used too give me hugs. They used to sing me songs. But then they stopped.

Jean: When did they stop?

Susan: When I was nine. I remember because I had a birthday party and lots of friends came. I didn't have any parties after that and all my friends went away. And I got fat. And they stopped putting me to bed. They'd give me a hug and a kiss when they put me to bed, but they don't put me to bed anymore. You do. And then you just turn out the light.

(Pause.)

Jean: That's when the fairies came.

Susan: Mmm…

(Pause.)

Jean: Susan, I'm so, so sorry.

(He leans down to her in the bath and kisses her forehead.)

Susan: You don't have to. Not if it doesn't feel nice.

Jean: It does feel nice.

(Susan splashes him. Jean splashes her back.)

Jean: Where did you come from?

(In the living room Holly has arrived.)

Mother: Who are you?

Holly: I'm Holly.

Mother: Bill, do you know this girl?

Father: Yes. She's a Muslim floozy. A friend of Jean's.

Mother: Jean has a friend? A girlfriend?

Father: I'm as baffled.

Holly: Is Jean here?

Mother: What do you do? Do you kiss him?

Holly: That's a little personal isn't it?

Mother: Well what makes you his girlfriend?

Holly: I watch him paint.

(Pause.)

Mother: He's in the bathroom. Be careful he might be naked. He smells too.

Holly: Thanks.

(She makes her way to the bathroom.)

Holly: Jean?

Jean: Hi. What are you doing here?

Holly: I haven't seen you for a while. I missed watching you paint. I thought you might be dead.

Susan: He is dead.

(Holly sees Susan in the bath.)

Susan: I'm fat and ugly and stupid.

Jean: Susan.

Holly: I'm skinny and sexy and smart.

Susan: I wish I was.

Holly: It doesn't mean much.

(Pause.)

Susan: Do you want to have a bath with us?

Holly: I'm okay.
(To Jean.) Your skin.

Jean: I'm decaying.

Holly: Do you want me to stay here till it's finished?

Jean: I think so.

Susan: You can stay.

Holly: Will your parents mind?

Jean: They're lost.

(Pause. Holly touches Jean's sores gently.)

Susan: Are you a fairy?

(Pause.)

Holly: Yeah.

Scene 2

Police station.

Father: So you see, it was extortion. It was illegal, surely. It was an illegal breaking of the law. Isn't that right?

Garda: Well, it depends.

Father: What does it depend on?

Garda: It depends on the amount of money involved.

Father: Why does it? In for a penny, in for a pound, Gard. If he was trying to stroke me for a pound, it would be the same as ripping me off for five hundred pounds. Would it not?

Garda: Well it's a moot point.

Father: How the hell is it a moot point?

Garda: We don't operate in pounds anymore.

Father: I know that. That's beside the point.

Garda: Beside the moot point?

Father: It's not a moot point.

Garda: But there are no pounds. You've obviously got your facts wrong.

Father: It doesn't matter. It's just a saying.

Garda: A what?

Father: A saying. Like a proverb. That's all. To illustrate a point.

(Pause.)

Garda: To illustrate a moot point?

Father: It's not moot, for Christ's sake.

Garda: Now there's no need to take the Lord's name in vain.

Father: But the fact is…

Garda: Now look here, Mr…

Father: Bill.

Garda: Look Bill. There is no point in perpetuating these old sayings while the currency all the while has changed. The saying is hopelessly outdated. We have the Euro now.

Father: Well in for a cent in for a Euro then.

Garda: Now that just sounds silly.

Father: But…

Garda: Let me illustrate a point for you, Bill. Your saying is gone. It is outdated. The practice of honest trade has gone the same way as your saying. What kind of place would I be running here if I pursued every case of some plonker trying to make a little dough on the side? It'd be feckin ridiculous.

Father: But that's your job!

Garda: I want you to listen to me very carefully. Your proverb is outdated. The currency in your proverb is outdated. Your expectations of trade practices are outdated. Your name is rarely used anymore…

Father: My name!

Garda: Bill. It's an old name. It's all washed up.
Now listen to me closely. Do you own your home?

Father: I would have finished paying it off next year if I hadn't been swindled out of my job.

Garda: What's it worth?

Father: What?

Garda: What's it worth. Come on, don't bullshit me. What's it worth.

(Pause.)

Father: One point four million.

Garda: One point four feckin million yo yos. And you're talking about someone making a few bucks on the sly. What did you buy it for? Twenty feckin shillings or something?

You're doing just fine.

Father: But why should he get what I earned? He's wealthier than me by a country mile.

Garda: Kilometer.

(Pause.)

Father: You're not going to help me are you?

Garda: How much was he trying to fuck you for?

Father: Forty thousand.

Garda: Bring me twenty and I'll sort it out for you.

(Pause. Father rubs his face with his hands.)

Father: I'm not going to give you a bribe.

Garda: It's a fee.

Father: I pay tax. I'm not going to pay you a fee.
I want to speak to your superior.

Garda: Sure. I'll just get him.
(Calling.) Seamus?

(The Gard goes. He does not return. Eventually father slowly rises and exits.)

Scene 3

(Jean in the bar.)

Bartender: How do you drink so much and not get drunk?

Jean: It's a party trick.

Bartender: Why are you here? I've never seen you here without your da.

Jean: I need to ask you something and tell you something.

Bartender: Okay. Fire away.

Jean: Are you the woman my father loves?

(Pause.)

Jean: That's the thing I need to ask. That's the first part of it.

(Pause.)

Jean: I'd like you to answer me. I need to know.

Bartender: Why?

Jean: Because I don't know anything. I think I should know something or other. Even if it's just something small.

Bartender: Yes.

Jean: Yes. Yes you are his love?

Bartender: I'm sorry Jean. Sometimes things don't go the way you plan…

Jean: Don't bullshit me. And don't treat me like a child.

Bartender: Very well. When he walked into this bar fifteen years ago it was like two ropes flew out of our chests and tangled themselves between us. And that's the way it's been ever since.

Do you want to know anything else?

Jean: No.

Bartender: There was something you wanted to tell me.

Jean: He's dying of cancer.

(The bartender weeps softly and barely perceptably.)

Bartender: When will he die?

Jean: Soon. No one knows when. It's pancreas, so it won't be long.

(Pause.)

Bartender: Why did you tell me?

Jean: Because he is going to die without love. You are all that loves him.

Bartender: What about you?

Jean: I'll be leaving soon.

Bartender: Where are you going?

Jean: To the river.

Bartender: I see.

I can't go to his house. Will you tell him to come to me?

Jean: I will. But it may be too late.

Bartender: Jean…

Jean: Yes?

Bartender: Why is there such sadness?

Jean: I don't know. I don't know very much at all. I have to go home. *(Pause. He turns to leave.)* Perhaps because the heart is never full. And the empty part is massively empty. *(Pause.)* My girlfriend is waiting there.

Bartender: Lucky you.

(Jean exits.)

Bartender: Come back.

Scene 4

Mother and Lover.

Mother: I'm sorry I've been so rude and blunt.

Lover: I don't care.

Mother: But it's not right. And not nice.

Lover: You don't understand. I'm in love with you. I don't care.

Mother: Don't let people walk on you. My husband does that. It's not attractive.

Lover: People will walk on you anyway.

Mother: I suppose so.

(Pause.)

Mother: My husband has decided to accept things as they are.

Lover: That's good.

Mother: He wants us to be able to be together if we want to. Whenever. Even under his roof. He wants us to be happy.

Lover: That's good.

Mother: He's given up.

Lover: Perhaps he's tired.

Mother: He's given up his dignity.

Lover: He's tired.

Mother: He wants us all to have dinner together. He's going to cook his favorite soup and a lamb roast.

Lover: I don't eat meat.

Mother: I'll tell him. He'll fix you something nice. He really wants to do this.

Lover: You've never done what he wanted before.

(Pause.)

Mother: I know.

Lover: Then why now?

Mother: Because he's trying.
Will you come to dinner?

Lover: If it will make you happy, I'll come to dinner.

(Pause.)

Lover: I think you love him still.

Mother: Jesus, you say some fucking stupid things sometimes.

Scene 5

Father and Uncle in Uncle's room.

Father: What have you done to my son?

Uncle: It was he who stole my spider. He was bitten.

(A pause.)

Uncle: Look at these vials of venom. This one cripples. This one kills in about six hours, this one kills in ten minutes, this one kills instantly and this one, this empty one is going to have the venom that kills before death knows it has arrived.

Father: That doesn't make any sense. Death can't precede itself. Death is death.

Uncle: Death is everywhere. All the time.

Father: No. Death is a moment. Death is an instant.

Uncle: Death is there from the moment of birth, working, functioning.

Father: You're insane.

Uncle: Your son is dead and decaying and yet he moves.

(Father lunges at the Uncle and throttles him. Uncle struggles and frees himself.)

Uncle: I did nothing. He's to blame for his own death. He decided on it.

Father: I'll kill you.

Uncle: Will you? If you do your wife will divorce you and take all your wealth with her.

Father: You think I care about that?

Uncle: Oh yes. Deep down you care. You care about it more than anything else including your son.

Father: Stay away from my children.

Uncle: Listen to me, Bill. This spider is loose in your house. It will kill. It will also evolve. If it evolves it will develop the ability to cause death with massive anguish attached to it. It will develop massive death, like the horrors of cancer multiplied by approximately twelve.

Father: You're a nut.

Uncle: Your cancer is nothing to compare to it. It will seize the lungs like a Jove. It will smash the stomach like a thunder clap. It will evolve to this.

Your son has been lucky. He decays and feels no pain. But when it has evolved, great pain will follow.

Father: Enough.

Uncle: Find it. Or we will all die.

Father: You will. There's no doubt about that.

Uncle: When will you let it go?

Father: What?

Uncle: Let it go. Join the world again.

Father: Join this sickness? This decay?

(Pause.)

Perhaps I will.

Scene 6

Holly holds Jean on the couch.

Jean: Doesn't the smell bother you?

Holly: No.

Jean: What do you see in me?

Holly: I don't know. The finishing line.

(Enter Cuchulain. He is tired.)

Jean: What do you want?

Holly: Nothing.

Jean: Cuchulain.

Holly: Oh. Is he here now?

Cuchulain: I'm tired. I'm more tired than when I raised my sword against the sea.

Jean: You fought the sea? With your sword?

Cuchulain. It's not such a stupid suggestion, is it? I won.

Jean: You won?

Cuchulain: Yes, I won. You should know all this. What did they teach you in school?

Jean: Trigonometry.

Cuchulain: What's that?

Jean: I don't know.
(Pause.)
Why did you raise your sword against the sea?

Cuchulain: I killed my son in battle. But I didn't know it was my son until it was too late.

Jean: Oh. I'm sorry.

Cuchulain: Thank you.

Jean: How was it the sea's fault?

Cuchulain: It wasn't.

Jean: Then why did you attack the sea?

(Pause.)

Cuchulain: I… I was angry.

Jean: Oh.

(Pause.)

Cuchulain: Is that your girl?

Jean: I guess.

Cuchulain: Do you love her?

Jean: No. I don't think so. I can't feel anything.

Cuchulain: Time for you to die.

Jean: I think so. I can't see the point of living if I can't feel anything.

Cuchulain: Now you see.

Jean: Yes.

(Enter Mother. Cuchulain exits.)

Mother: We're having a guest for dinner tonight. You have to go out.

Jean: Where will we go?

Mother: I don't know. Go to the movies. And take Susan with you.

Jean: Alright.

Mother: Chop chop.

Jean: What, now? Susan's sleeping. Her legs were hurting her.

Mother: Wake her up. Our guest will be here soon.

Jean: When can we come home?

Mother: Later. After midnight.

Jean: But Susan goes to bed at ten.

Mother: *(Suddenly screams.)* For fuck's sake Jean, get out of this house!

(Pause.)

Jean: All right.

(He goes to get Susan. Holly remains.)

Mother: You're crazy to be with him.

Holly: Don't you want him to be happy?

Mother: There's nothing left. It'll be the same for him. There isn't any hope.

Holly: I don't need hope.

Mother: Everyone needs hope. If you don't need anything else you need hope.

Holly: Hope for what?

Mother: Change.

Holly: Change from what?

Mother: Change to something better.

Holly: You have everything. What more could you want?

(Pause.)

Mother: You have all the answers don't you.

Holly: Your son knows you're having an affair.
(Pause.) He told me. He knows.

Mother: I don't care.

Holly: No?
Why do you hate him?

Mother: Because he hurt me.

(Jean returns with Susan.)

Susan: My legs hurt and I was asleep. Now I'm sleepy and sore. Where are we going?

Jean: A Good question, Susie.
Have a pleasant dinner, mother.

Mother: Don’t take Susan to a scary movie.

Jean: Why? Are you worried about her, or do you just not want to have to get up in the middle of the night to comfort her?

(She slaps him across the face.)

Jean: *(Pause. Rubbing his face.)* Hm. No pain.

(Jean, Holly and Susan exit together. Mother breaks into hysterical sobbing.)

Scene 7

The Fairies, hand in hand. Mother continues to sob aside.

Fairy 1: I don't want to be here anymore.

Fairy 2: Only a few more hours. Then we can take her away.

Fairy: Do you remember when the grass grew over our hands? When the vines tangled around our waists?

Fairy 2: I remember the lightest of days. I remember the freshest air and the sweet scent of spring in the heather. And the sun. Bright and warm.

Fairy 1: Where will we go?

Fairy 2: To the place that's far. And hide ourselves until the decaying is finished. For it will be then and only then that the air will once more be sweet and light.

Fairy1: I can smell it.

Fairies 1 and 2: Water, be my self cleansed with thee,
Water by the bowing tree,
Water by the river and the sea,
Water cometh, washeth over me.

(McManus enters and sits at a desk. Father enters through the faeries. McManus stands.)

McManus: No?

Father: I can't.

McManus: You mean you won't.

Father: Yes. That is what I mean.

(Father draws an enormous sword.)

Scene 8

Dinner. Uncle, Mother, Lover are sitting at the table. Father stands.

Sign: *The End of Things.*

Father: Well, my friends, here we are. I want to thank you all for coming.

I have brought us all together to address the obvious tensions between us and to dispel them over a meal and hearty red wine from a sunny French vineyard. Please enjoy your soup as I ramble.

(The guests eat as he speaks.)

It has become abundantly clear to me that the world around me has changed and I have failed to change with it. The country that my father bore on his back through rebellion and that I struggled to survive in has been replaced by a new, affluent society. It is a society of want and not of need. It is a society of growth and not of survival.

These are wonderful changes to our society. And with such changes comes changes in the behaviour of the human animal within it. It is these changes that I have struggled most to welcome, to embrace. And so tonight, I open myself to this new order. I wish to embrace all of ye who have become accustomed to this new order, and Scrooge-like, I wish to abandon my ill-conceived and outdated habits and notions and step aboard this new train of being with you all.

Brother-in-law. I have treated you poorly. Forgive me. I now would like to be included in your vile experiments to create death. I will learn to be fascinated by them and show interest in their development. Indeed I have already attempted by own clumsy efforts in this regard. Perhaps you will find the time to share your knowledge with me. On this you have my word.

(Uncle toasts silently in Father's direction.)

You, my good sir, are to be my new friend. You have found the affections of my wife and she has found yours. She would not have brought you here tonight if she were not serious about this. And so I accept that she no longer requires or desires my affections and prefers your. There is no point in me bucking this new situation and so I accept you and enfold you into my home. You may come and go as you please and need not feel the need to fuck my wife behind my back. I know what's going on and I have swallowed and digested it. Welcome, sir.

(Lover toasts silently in his direction.)

To you, my good wife, we have seen good and bad times. We have fought. We have attempted the ridiculous proposition of sustaining our love for thirty years. You have not felt that initial love for me for a long time, and this I accept. I require no affection or attention from you. I wish you only happiness should you choose to stay under my roof or not. Your desire for affection from this gentleman is entirely understandable as he is young and virile while I accept that I am outdated, over-weight and somewhat wrinkly. May your sex be good and may you look after each other's emotional fragility.

I want you to accept that I am utterly sincere in this. There is no choice for me. There is the desert of loneliness and perhaps suicide if I do not cop onto myself and move with the times. I wish to learn the arts of bribery, dishonesty, intrigue, so craftily practiced by our political and economic leaders, and if I am lucky, sluttery. I too will attempt to join this world by screwing as many people as I can out of money and having an affair with someone or other at some stage. Perhaps I can assist in the spread of some venereal disease.

It appears you have enjoyed your soup. There is a roast lamb to come. It shall take just a few minutes longer, and for you, good sir, there is a meal of exceptional roasted seasonal vegetables.

(Mother begins to cough and choke.)

What is it, dear? Are you unwell?

Mother: My throat is tightening. Constricting. I'm having trouble breathing.

Lover: Perhaps there was something in the soup you are allergic to.

Mother: I'm not allergic to anything.

Uncle: I too am feeling it… What soup was this?

Father: Leak and potato, my good Uncle.

Lover: Ug. I too am tightening around the collar. Are you sure it wasn't seafood? I am allergic to clams.

Father: No, no. It was leak and potato. Not a hint of seafood. This is terrible. This is ruining everything. Shall I call a doctor?

Mother: Yes. For God's sake, I can't breath.

Father: Well I could call a doctor, or I could let you all choke.

(Pause.)

Lover: What? Call a doctor. I can't get any air.

Father: Well I could. I suppose I should. But would that not be considerate? Would that be the way of the new order? I don't know.

Uncle: You must call a doctor immediately. We're suffocating.

Father: Yes. But really that compromises my new approach to living. That would be assisting someone in a time of trouble. That would be helping someone when a great invisible hand was slowly squeezing their neck. I don't know, my new friends. I just don't know.

Lover: You… You did this… You poisoned us.

Father: I did? I don't know about that. Poisoned is an outdated term. Envenomed might be a better term.

Uncle: The spider. The venom. You…

Father: *(Indicating the audience.)* It was behind the television of all places. It was spinning a web.

(Mother's head falls to the table and she lies gasping like a fish out of water.)

Father: But it seems to be working faster than you first assessed. It seems my first, clumsy experiments were not so clumsy after all. It should, according to the evolution of it, be causing you massive agony, greater than any cancerous attack. You should be in diabolical pain, and it seems you are.

(Lover also falls.)

Lover: *(Gasping.)* Fuck you. Fuck… you…

Father: Fuck me? No no, my new friend. No one will fuck me ever again. That's the new order. I'm going to fuck you before you can fuck me. I'm going to use you for my ends and then leave you to rot in your pain.

(Uncle falls.)

Father: Uncle, are you unwell?

Uncle: It has evolved. It is massive death. You've killed us.

Father: Indeed I have. But surely you've developed an anti-venom. There'd be a little vial of antidote in that hovel of an attic of yours, wouldn't there?

Uncle: *(Gasps but can no longer speak.)*

Father: Oh. Perhaps not. So you make it. *(He takes a jar with the spider in it from under his seat.)* But there's nothing to stop it if it falls into the wrong hands? What a shame.

(All the guests lie gasping. They can no longer speak.)

Father: Look at this creature. Never did any harm to anyone. And look what you've turned it into.

(He produces a syringe from his pocket.)

This is morphine. This was to be my future. Lying on a hospital bed surrounded by vampires, being pumped full of this heroin to make things seem less dreadful. Can I offer it to you? There's only enough for one.

(The others try to reach for the morphine, try to speak, but cannot.)

No? No takers?

(He injects himself.)

Well, I wouldn't want to see it go to waste. There are people starving in Africa.

(He sits and makes himself comfortable.)

Now, if you don't mind, I shall quietly enjoy my soup. And after I have finished I will meet you in hell. How does that sound?

(He eats. The rest die. A time lapse in which Cuchulain enters and goes to Father. He gently places his head slowly onto the table.)

All are dead around the table. The fairies stand by. Jean, Susan and Holly enter. Jean immediately lies on the floor. Holly goes to the figures at the table.)

Holly: They're dead.

Susan: Mammy is dead?

Holly: Mammy is dead.

Susan: Right so.

Jean: It's time for me.

Holly: Do you want me to hold your hand?

Jean: Yes.

(Holly goes to him and takes his hand.)

Jean: Susan.

Susan: Yes?

Jean: Where will you go?

Susan: With the fairies.

Jean: Go then.

Fairy 1: Come.

Susan: Is it a long way? My legs might hurt.

Fairy 2: It is a long way. But your legs won't hurt.

Jean: I'll meet you there.

Susan: At the Boyne?

Jean: At the Boyne.

Susan: Are you coming?

Jean: I'll meet you at the bank where the green trees grow. Will we have a bath in the Boyne?

Susan: Yes. I'd like that. Maybe we'll see the smart fish.

Jean: Go now.

(The Fairies take Susan away. Jean dies. Holly lets his hand go and stands. She picks up the jar with the spider from Father's place at the table. She looks at it for a moment. She takes off the lid and carefully lies the jar on its side. She backs carefully away and exits as the spider escapes. The Bartender enters. She looks around her at the devastation, goes to father and touches his face. Cuchulain's head drops. Darkness comes.)

END

www.ingramcontent.com/pod-product-compliance
Ingram Content Group UK Ltd.
Pitfield, Milton Keynes, MK11 3LW, UK
UKHW041941190726
13854UKWH00004B/1720